S is for School!

By P.J. Shaw
Illustrated by Joe Mathieu

Dalmatian Press, LLC, 2006. All rights reserved.
Published by Dalmatian Press, LLC, 2006. The DALMATIAN PRESS name and logo are trademarks of Dalmatian
Press, LLC, Franklin, Tennessee 37067. No part of this book may be reproduced or copied in any form without
written permission from the copyright owner.

Printed in the U.S.A.
ISBN: 1-40372-346-X (X) 1-40372-737-6 (M)

06 07 08 09 LBM 10 9 8 7 6 5 4 3 2 1
15304 Sesame Street 8x8 Storybook: S is for School!

Hello, Dorothy!
Today was Elmo's
first day of school.
What's that, Dorothy?
You want to know
what it's like on
the very first day
of school? Elmo
will tell you.

The first day of school is *so* exciting!

Just getting there is an adventure!

Some monsters wonder what to do on the first day of school.

At school, you might feel a little lonely now and then.

But a smile helps you make new friends.
A smile—and some crayons!

On the first day of school, a little fish can get homesick... so bring a picture for company. Guess what? Elmo brings a picture of Dorothy!

On the first day of school you see lots of new faces.

Lots of *friendly* faces! Yay!

The *end* of the first day of school is exciting, too.

It's a good time
for sharing what you've learned...

...with a friend!